nee
P6

The Wedding Gift Goof

When Nancy got home, there was a message waiting for her: "Call Bess right away."

Nancy carried the portable phone up to her room to call Bess. "Hi," Nancy said. "What's up?"

"Something terrible," Bess said. Her voice was shaking. "Remember that envelope that had the money for the wedding gift?"

"Yes," Nancy answered. "What's wrong?"

"It's gone!" Bess cried.

The Nancy Drew Notebooks

\# 1 The Slumber Party Secret

\# 2 The Lost Locket

\# 3 The Secret Santa

\# 4 Bad Day for Ballet

\# 5 The Soccer Shoe Clue

\# 6 The Ice Cream Scoop

\# 7 Trouble at Camp Treehouse

\# 8 The Best Detective

\# 9 The Thanksgiving Surprise

#10 Not Nice on Ice

#11 The Pen Pal Puzzle

#12 The Puppy Problem

#13 The Wedding Gift Goof

Available from MINSTREL Books

#13

THE NANCY DREW NOTEBOOKS®

THE WEDDING GIFT GOOF

CAROLYN KEENE

Illustrated by Anthony Accardo

A MINSTREL® BOOK

PUBLISHED BY POCKET BOOKS

New York   London   Toronto   Sydney   Tokyo   Singapore

A MINSTREL PAPERBACK *Original*

 A Minstrel Book published by
POCKET BOOKS, a division of Simon & Schuster Inc.
1230 Avenue of the Americas, New York, NY 10020

Copyright © 1996 by Simon & Schuster Inc.
Produced by Mega-Books Inc.

ISBN: 0-671-53552-8

First Minstrel Books printing July 1996

10 9 8 7 6 5 4 3 2 1

Cover art by Aleta Jenks

Printed in the U.S.A.

THE
WEDDING GIFT GOOF

1

Ms. Spencer's Secret

Guess what?" Bess Marvin gasped. "We're getting a new teacher! A man!"

Eight-year-old Nancy Drew frowned. "How do you know?" she asked.

"That's him," Bess said. She pointed to a man in the school playground. He was standing beside their third-grade teacher, Ms. Spencer. The man had curly black hair and a dimple in his chin.

Bess pushed her long blond hair out of her face. "I don't want a new teacher. Not now—not ever! Ms. Spencer is the best."

Nancy was about to agree. But just

then George Fayne ran up to join them. George's curly dark hair bounced as she ran. She was Bess's cousin and Nancy's other best friend.

"What's wrong with you two?" George asked. "You look upset."

"We're getting a new teacher," Bess repeated. "A man."

George put her hands on her hips. "Who told you?" she asked Bess.

"Well," Bess said slowly. "It's just a rumor. I *guess* it might not be true. . . ."

George pointed a finger at her cousin. "Who told you?" she asked again.

Bess's cheeks turned a little pink. "It was Brenda Carlton," she admitted.

"Brenda Carlton?" Nancy asked. Her eyes opened wide. Brenda was the most gossipy girl in the third grade.

"I wouldn't believe anything Brenda says," George said with a laugh. "She makes up stories all the time."

"I know," Bess said. "But Brenda promises it's true. She heard Ms. Spencer talking to him. Ms. Spencer said, 'I haven't told the class yet.' And then she said something about leaving."

Nancy turned to watch her teacher carefully. Ms. Spencer and the man were looking at a piece of paper. Nancy wasn't sure what the paper was. She thought it might be a list.

"She *has* been acting weird lately," George said. "She whispers to the other teachers all the time."

"And she's been writing something secret," Bess said.

"You're right," Nancy said. "Something is going on. I'm going to see if I can find out what."

Nancy straightened her bright blue sweatshirt. Then she tightened the matching blue scrunchie in her hair. It held her reddish blond hair in a ponytail.

I don't want my new teacher to see me looking sloppy, Nancy thought.

"Should we come with you?" George asked.

Nancy shook her head. "Wait here."

As soon as she neared Ms. Spencer and the man, Nancy slowed down.

I can't just walk right up to them, Nancy thought. Maybe I can see what's on that paper if I stand on something.

Nancy looked around. There was a tire swing nearby. She walked toward the swing. But just as she reached for it, Mike Minelli ran up and grabbed it by the chain.

"Ha, ha. Got here first," Mike called as he climbed on the tire.

He started swinging as hard as he could. He came much too close to Nancy. She jumped out of the way.

Nancy crossed her arms and turned around. She marched back toward George and Bess. They ran to meet her.

"I saw that," Bess said. "What a creep!"

"I don't care," Nancy said. "I couldn't see the paper from there anyway. It was too far away."

Just then the bell rang. Everyone started running toward the door.

"Come on," Nancy said, smiling. "Let's go in. We have a mystery to solve."

"A mystery?" a voice near Nancy said. Nancy looked over and saw Rebecca Ramirez. She was walking right behind Nancy, Bess, and George. "What mystery?"

"We're getting a new teacher," Bess answered.

Instantly, Rebecca put her hands up to her face. "Oh, no!" Rebecca cried. "How awful for you."

Nancy smiled. Rebecca wanted to be an actress when she grew up. She always acted *very* dramatic.

Very happy. *Very* sad. *Very* upset. About everything.

"How can you stand it?" Rebecca said, grabbing Nancy's arm.

"We don't know if it's true," Nancy said. "It's just a rumor. But we're going to find out."

"Well, let me know after school," Rebecca said. Then she hurried to her own third-grade class.

Nancy and her friends moved quickly through the hallway.

"I'm going to stand at the pencil sharpener by Ms. Spencer's desk," Bess announced. "Maybe I can get a look at that paper when she puts it on her desk."

"Okay," Nancy agreed. "George and I will try to get Ms. Spencer's attention."

But as soon as Nancy took her seat, Ms. Spencer walked in. The paper was in her hand. Bess didn't have time to go to the pencil sharpener.

"Class, take your seats please," Ms. Spencer said. "I have something to tell you all."

Uh-oh, Nancy thought. Here it comes.

Nancy felt her throat get tight. She didn't want a new teacher. Ms. Spencer was the best teacher Nancy had ever had.

"Please quiet down, everyone," Ms.

Spencer said. She walked around to sit on the edge of her desk.

The class got quiet very quickly. I know what you're going to say, Nancy thought.

"I have something very important to tell you," Ms. Spencer said, smiling. "Something very nice. In a few weeks, I'm getting married. And you're all invited to the wedding!"

2

Wedding Plans

Getting married?" Nancy said, her eyes lighting up.

Nancy glanced over at Bess, who sat beside her in class. Bess's own eyes were big.

"A wedding," Bess whispered, clapping her hands together. "Goody!"

"Oh, no," George said, rolling her eyes. "I can see it all now. Bess thinks she's in charge."

Nancy laughed, and everyone in the class began talking at once.

Mike Minelli turned around and started singing "Here Comes the

Bride." Jason Hutchings made very loud kissing sounds with his lips.

"Class, settle down," Ms. Spencer said, still smiling.

Nancy squirmed in her seat. A wedding. It was so exciting!

Ms. Spencer was probably marrying the man with the curly dark hair, Nancy thought. He wasn't a new teacher. He was Ms. Spencer's fiancé.

Nancy liked the word *fiancé*. It was French. It meant the person you were getting married to.

Ms. Spencer reached into her desk and took out a stack of thick, cream-colored envelopes.

"These are wedding invitations," she said as she started down the aisle. "One for each of you."

When she had passed out the invitations, Ms. Spencer sat on her desk again. She answered questions about the wedding. She said her fiancé's name was Martin Reynolds and that after the wedding she would be called Mrs. Reynolds.

Finally it was time for art class. Ms. Spencer walked the class down to Ms. Frick's art room. It was in the basement.

"I have an idea," Bess whispered on the way. "Let's give Ms. Spencer a party. A surprise party."

"A party?" George said softly.

"Yes, in school," Bess said. "On the day before her wedding."

"Great idea," Nancy said.

"Hey, that *is* a great idea," Lindsay Mitchell said. Lindsay was eavesdropping on Nancy's conversation. As usual. "We can have cake and punch."

"Shhh!" Bess said. "Ms. Spencer will hear." Bess lowered her voice, and the girls huddled together.

"We can buy her a gift," Bess went on. "A silver tea set."

Lindsay laughed quietly. "No way," she said. "Silver things cost too much."

"Okay, then how about a lace tablecloth?" Bess said. "Or maybe a punch bowl?"

"Let's ask Ms. Frick to help us decide," Nancy whispered. "And she can help with the party, too. Maybe we can make a big card for Ms. Spencer in art."

George nodded and Lindsay agreed. Bess's eyes twinkled as she bounced into the art room.

"Guess what?" Bess said to Ms. Frick. "Ms. Spencer is getting married—and we're invited to the wedding."

Ms. Frick put her hand on Bess's shoulder and bent down. "I know!" she said, sounding just as excited as Bess.

"We want to give her a surprise party," Bess announced.

Ms. Frick smiled and cocked her head to one side. Her long earrings dangled back and forth. Ms. Frick was tall and had short, wavy brown hair. Nancy thought her colorful clothes and jewelry looked just right for an artist.

"What a good idea," Ms. Frick said. "A surprise party. Class, do you think you can all keep a secret?"

Everyone settled down when they heard the word "party." Then Nancy told Ms. Frick about her idea to make a huge card.

"We could make it look like a giant wedding cake. And we could decorate it with all kinds of fancy colors—like icing," Nancy said.

Ms. Frick nodded. "And inside, each person could write a poem. Or a message. Or draw a picture of himself or herself," the art teacher added.

By the time class was over, everything had been decided. The surprise party would be on the Friday before Ms. Spencer's wedding. Everyone in the class was going to chip in. Bess would collect the money and give it to Ms. Frick to keep. Then Bess's mother would buy the present.

The class had voted to get Ms. Spencer a special cookie jar shaped like a schoolhouse. The cookie jar was George's idea. She had seen it in a gift shop.

"I still think we should get her a tablecloth," Bess said after school that day.

George rolled her eyes.

"Get who a tablecloth?" Rebecca Ramirez asked. She walked up to join Nancy, Bess, and George outside.

"Ms. Spencer isn't leaving our school after all," Nancy said. "She's getting married. And our whole class is invited to the wedding."

Rebecca dropped her books on the sidewalk with a thud. Her eyes grew big. "A wedding? You're going to a wedding?" she said.

Nancy nodded.

"Well, you'd better come over to my house right now," Rebecca said. "I'll tell you everything. What to wear. Where to sit. How to catch the bride's bouquet. I know, because I went to my cousin's wedding last year."

"We already know *all* about it," Bess said quickly. "A friend of my mom's got married when I was six years old. I was the flower girl."

"Oh, but this is different," Rebecca said. "This is your *teacher's* wedding. And anyway, being a flower girl isn't the same thing as being a guest."

"Why not?" Bess asked, tossing her hair over her shoulders.

"Because," Rebecca said with a huge sigh. "You have to *know* things. Like where to sit in the church. In this case, you should sit on the left, because you are a friend of the bride. The friends of the groom sit on the right."

Bess rolled her eyes and glanced at Nancy. George made a face, too. Nancy gave them a small smile. But she also nodded at Rebecca.

"I'd love to come over," Nancy said. "But I'm getting a ride home with Bess and George today. Bess's mom is taking us to the library."

"Oh," Rebecca said. "Okay. Well, don't worry. I'll make a list of things you need to know about weddings. I'll give it to you tomorrow morning on the way to school."

The next day Nancy walked to school with Rebecca. Rebecca handed Nancy a sheet of pink paper. It said "All About Weddings" in pencil at the top.

"Read it as soon as you can," Rebecca told Nancy. "Then meet me after school and we can talk about it."

"Okay," Nancy agreed.

"I wish I were in Ms. Spencer's class," Rebecca called as she headed toward her own classroom. "But even though I'm not, I'm going to get her a present. Crystal candlesticks. Your class should get her something nice, too."

Nancy sighed. Rebecca was her friend, but sometimes it made Nancy tired just talking to her. She thought

she knew more than anyone about everything.

After school Nancy, Bess, and George stood in front of the building. Nancy showed the All About Weddings paper to Bess and George.

"This is dumb," Bess said. "Everyone knows that the bride feeds the first piece of cake to the groom. Why did she write that down for you?"

"I don't know," Nancy said. "I think she wants to go to the wedding, too."

"Well, where is she?" Bess said, staring at the school door. "If she wants to talk about the wedding so much, why isn't she here?"

Just then the school door opened. Rebecca ran out. She had a serious look on her face. Her long black hair was flowing behind her.

"I have horrible news," Rebecca said, looking very upset. "Horrible. Get ready."

"What? What's wrong?" Nancy asked.

"The wedding is off!" Rebecca said.

3

Wedding Woes

No!" Nancy gasped. "No wedding? But why?"

Nancy glanced at Bess and George. They looked just as shocked as she was.

"I heard Ms. Spencer talking to Ms. Frick," Rebecca said. "She said, 'I never liked him much anyway.' And then she said that the wedding was off."

"No fair," Bess said, stamping her foot. "Now we can't have our party."

"I don't know," Nancy said slowly. "Are you sure, Rebecca?"

"Well, I'm just telling you what I heard," Rebecca said.

Nancy looked at the kids streaming out of the school. It wasn't hard for Nancy to spot Ms. Frick in the crowd.

"Ms. Frick?" Nancy called, running toward the art teacher. Bess, George, and Rebecca chased after her. "May we ask you something?"

Ms. Frick stopped on the walkway. "Sure, girls. What's wrong?"

Nancy quickly told her what Rebecca had said about Ms. Spencer calling off her wedding.

Ms. Frick shook her head. "Girls, you have to be careful about eavesdropping," she said. "That's a good way to start rumors. And rumors can be all wrong."

"But I *heard* her say the wedding was off," Rebecca insisted.

"Yes," Ms. Frick said, nodding. "But Ms. Spencer was talking about her *cousin's* wedding, not her own. She said she never liked her *cousin's* boyfriend. That's why she didn't mind that the wedding was called off. See?"

Nancy nodded. Rebecca blushed. And Bess clapped her hands together.

"So the wedding is still on?" George asked, just to be sure.

"Yes," Ms. Frick said. "And so is our surprise party. So *shhhh*. Let's keep it a secret."

For the next two weeks, Nancy and the rest of Ms. Spencer's class worked on planning the party. Nancy was proud of the wedding cake card, because it was her idea. It was big—bigger than a card sold in a store. There were swirling lace decorations on the front. The lace looked like fancy icing. On top were the figures of a bride and groom.

Bess and Nancy bought new dresses to wear to the wedding. Even George, who didn't like fancy clothes at all, got a new ribbon for her hair.

Finally the week of the wedding arrived. After school on Wednesday, Bess,

Nancy, and George went to Ms. Frick's room to pick up the envelope of money.

"Be careful with this," Ms. Frick said. She handed a bulging white envelope to Bess. "We have fifty dollars in there."

"Oh, I'll be careful," Bess promised. "I'll give it to my mom right away. She's picking me up from school."

"Good," Ms. Frick said.

Nancy and George followed Bess out to the parking lot. Mrs. Marvin's red minivan was parked near the playground. Two boys were sitting in the van. Mrs. Marvin stood outside.

"Hi, sweetie," Mrs. Marvin said to Bess. "Hello, girls. Could you wait just a moment? I need to talk to some other mothers about the food for the party on Friday."

"Okay," Bess said. "Here." She handed the white envelope full of money to her mother.

"Thanks, sweetie." Mrs. Marvin opened the passenger door to the van

and leaned in. Then she stuck the white envelope into her purse. Nancy could see that Mrs. Marvin's purse was standing open on the floor between the two front seats. A big brown padded envelope and a few other packages were there, too.

"Is that the money for the gift?" a voice behind Nancy asked.

Nancy, Bess, and George whirled around. Rebecca was standing behind them.

"Yes," Bess said. "Why?"

"Oh, I just wondered how much you collected," Rebecca said. "Because I still think you should get her something nicer than a cookie jar. Something like I'm getting. Crystal candlesticks, for instance."

"You're really getting her candlesticks?" Bess asked. Her mouth fell open. "You're not even in our class."

Rebecca didn't answer. Instead, she stared past the girls into Bess's car.

"Hey, I didn't know you were friends

with Greg Karoli," she said, pointing into the backseat. "I heard he's taking acting lessons. He's practically famous!"

Bess looked over her shoulder quickly, then turned back to Rebecca.

"We're not really friends. He's in fourth grade. His mother is friends with my mom, so we're giving him a ride home."

"Who's that other guy?" Rebecca said. "Look, he's messing up your seats!"

Nancy, Bess, and George all looked this time. Rebecca was right. A boy named Josh Lemon was in the minivan, too. He was climbing all over the seats, trying to get Greg's backpack away from him.

"That's Josh," Bess answered. "Hey, cut it out!" she called.

"I'll make them stop," Rebecca said. "I want to talk to Greg about his acting lessons anyway."

Rebecca walked over to the side door

of the minivan. She climbed partway in. The boys kept horsing around. Josh climbed over the middle seat to wrestle with Greg.

"She is so bossy," Bess whispered.

"Bess is right," George said. "I'm sick of her telling us what to do about Ms. Spencer's wedding."

"Oh, she's just jealous," Nancy said.

A few minutes later, Rebecca got out of the van. She came back to where Bess, Nancy, and George were standing.

"Those guys are jerks," Rebecca said to Bess. "Greg wouldn't even talk to me. Come on, Nancy. Let's go."

"Go where?" Nancy asked.

"Home, of course," Rebecca said.

"Oh, I forgot to tell you," Nancy said. "I'm not walking home today. Bess's mom is giving me a ride to my dad's office."

"Oh," Rebecca said. She looked disappointed. "Well, see you tomorrow."

Bess and George got into the van.

Nancy waved goodbye to Rebecca. Then she climbed into the van, too. Nancy sat next to Josh in the first row. Josh made a silly face at Nancy. Greg barely said hello. He just sat in the backseat and looked out the window.

Ten minutes later Mrs. Marvin dropped Nancy off at her dad's office. Nancy did her homework there. Then Nancy and her dad went home.

When they arrived, there was a message waiting for Nancy.

"Call Bess," Hannah Gruen said. "Right away."

Hannah was the Drew family's housekeeper. She had lived with Nancy and her father ever since Nancy was three years old.

Nancy picked up the portable phone in the living room. She carried it up to her room to call Bess. "Hi," Nancy said. "What's up?"

"Something terrible," Bess said. Her

voice was shaking. "Remember that envelope that had the money for the wedding gift?"

"Yes," Nancy answered. "What's wrong?"

"It's gone!" Bess cried.

4

No Money, No Gift

What do you mean?" Nancy said. "How can the money be gone?"

"I don't know," Bess said. "But it is. It's gone. When we got home, my mom looked in her purse, and the envelope was missing."

"Hold on," Nancy said, putting the phone down on her bedspread.

She ran to her desk and opened a drawer. Inside was a special blue notebook—the one she kept notes in when she was trying to solve a mystery.

Nancy grabbed the notebook and a pencil and hurried back to her bed.

"Okay," Nancy said. "Tell me everything. Where did you go after you dropped me at my dad's office?"

"Oh," Bess said. "Um . . . let me think. First we took Greg and Josh to Greg's house. Then we went to the post office. We had to mail a package to my grandmother. Then we came home."

Nancy was silent for a moment. She opened her notebook to a clean page. At the top she wrote:

Ms. Spencer's Wedding Gift Money

Then she wrote:

Envelope—Mrs. Marvin's purse—in car. Drove to Greg's house. Drove to post office.

"You didn't go *anywhere* else?" Nancy asked. "Try to think."

"I *am* thinking," Bess said, sounding upset. "Someone stole the money from my mom's purse. And I know who it was. It had to be one of those creepy boys."

"Maybe," Nancy said. She doodled a picture of the envelope in her notebook. Then she wrote:

Ms. Spencer's wedding—Saturday!!!!!

"We've got to find the money before the party," Bess said. "We've only got two days!"

"I know," Nancy said.

"My mom called Ms. Frick and told her about it," Bess went on. "My mom offered to buy the present with our own money. She said she feels like it's her fault."

"It's not her fault," Nancy said.

"I know," Bess agreed. "But the money was in my mom's purse. So she feels it's her job to make up for it. But Ms. Frick said no. She said that if someone stole the money, that person should give it back. Also, she didn't

want everyone talking about the stolen money. She said Ms. Spencer might hear about it. It would spoil the surprise."

That was true, Nancy thought.

"Okay," Nancy said. "Let's make a list of suspects. I'm writing Greg's name in my notebook right now. And Josh. He was in the car, too."

"Right," Bess said. "It's got to be one of them."

"Well . . . ," Nancy said slowly. "There is one other person."

"Who?" Bess asked.

"I hate to say it," Nancy said. "But it could have been Rebecca. She was in the car, remember?"

"Do you really think so?" Bess asked, sounding surprised.

Nancy thought about it for a minute. "Ummm . . . maybe yes, maybe no," she finally said. "I don't think she'd steal anything. But still, she's been acting really jealous lately. Maybe she took the money so she could buy those crystal candlesticks."

"Put her name down," Bess said firmly.

Nancy wrote Rebecca's name on the list in her notebook.

"There's one other thing," Bess said. "My mom searched the car. And guess what she found? A book. With Ned Nickerson's name in it."

Ned Nickerson? Nancy thought. He was a fourth-grade boy, too. Nancy had always liked Ned. He didn't tease her just because she was younger. Nancy didn't think he would steal anything.

"Was he in the car today?" Nancy asked Bess.

"I didn't see him," Bess replied. "But we weren't watching the whole time. He could have been."

"What kind of book is it?" Nancy asked.

"Oh, some mystery," Bess answered. "It's about two brothers who are detectives. I read a few pages. It looked like a really good story."

"Okay," Nancy announced. "I'm going to call Greg and ask him if he saw the money."

"My mom already called," Bess said. "But he wasn't home. She called Josh and Ned, too."

"What did they say?" Nancy asked.

"Nothing," Bess said. "They weren't home either."

"Okay," Nancy said. "I'll call them all."

"But *please* don't tell *anyone* that the money is missing, okay?" Bess said.

"Why not?" Nancy asked.

"Because," Bess said, "everyone will blame me. There was fifty dollars in that envelope—and now it's gone. People will think it's my fault."

"I'll try not to tell them," Nancy promised before hanging up.

A few minutes later, Nancy sat cross-legged on her bed. She looked up Josh's, Greg's, and Ned's phone numbers. She dialed Josh's number first. No answer.

Then she called Ned, but he wasn't home.

Finally she called Greg's phone number.

"Hello," Nancy said. "May I please speak to Greg?"

"I'm sorry," Greg's mom said. "But he's not here right now. He went out with his father to buy a new pair of in-line skates. May I take a message?"

"Uh, no thank you," Nancy said. Then she hung up.

In-line skates? Nancy thought. They're expensive.

I wonder where he got the money for them.

5

Thanks a Lot, Rebecca

Good morning, Pudding Pie," Nancy's father said as she hurried into the kitchen the next morning. "Want a ride to school today?"

"No thanks, Daddy," Nancy said. "Not today. I need to walk to school with Rebecca. She's one of my suspects."

"Suspects?" Carson Drew repeated. His eyebrows went up. "Are you trying to solve a new mystery?"

"Yes," Nancy said, nodding. "And you can help. How much do in-line skates cost, Daddy?"

"Oh, probably about fifty dollars," Carson Drew said, "or more."

Fifty dollars? Nancy thought. That's exactly how much money was in the envelope.

"What's going on?" Carson Drew asked.

"Tell you later," Nancy said.

She ate her oatmeal quickly. Hannah had put raisins and brown sugar in it. Then Nancy grabbed her books and her lunch. With a quick goodbye to her father and Hannah, she hurried out the door.

Rebecca was waiting for her at the corner.

"Hi!" Rebecca said, waving.

"Hi," Nancy called back.

Then the two girls started walking to school.

"Listen," Nancy said. "I want to ask you something. When you were in Bess's car yesterday, did you see that envelope full of money?"

"Why?" Rebecca asked. "Is it gone?"

Nancy's eyes opened wide. "How did you know?"

"I just guessed," Rebecca said.

"Yes, the money is gone," Nancy admitted. "Did you see it?"

Rebecca shook her head solemnly. "No," she said. "But if the money is gone, then you can't get Ms. Spencer a gift. And it's all Bess's fault!"

"That's not true," Nancy said.

"Poor Ms. Spencer," Rebecca went on. "She *was* going to get a party and a cookie jar. And now—*nothing.*"

"Oh, don't be silly," Nancy said. "We'll still have the party."

Rebecca shook her head sadly. "Yes, but you won't have a present for her. So your whole party's going to be ruined."

Thanks a lot, Rebecca! Nancy thought.

At recess girls started coming up to Bess.

"Did you get the present yet?" Amara Shane wanted to know.

"Is it pretty? Did you get silver-and-

39

white wrapping paper?" Lindsay asked. "My mom always uses silver paper for weddings."

"How big is it?" Brenda Carlton asked.

Bess bit her fingernails. She didn't know what to say.

George stepped in to rescue Bess.

"Quit bugging her about it," George said. "Bess's mom didn't get the present yet. But she'll get it tonight."

"Well, she'd *better* get it tonight," Lindsay said. "The party is tomorrow."

"Don't worry," George said. "Everything will be fine by tomorrow."

I hope you're right, Nancy thought. She saw that George had her fingers crossed behind her back.

"Nancy," Bess said when the three girls were alone, "do you have any clues yet?"

"No," Nancy said, "but I have some ideas."

"Like what?" George asked.

"Like him," Nancy said, pointing to Ned Nickerson.

Ned was tossing a baseball back and forth with another fourth-grade boy.

"I want to ask him something," Nancy said. "Be right back."

Nancy jogged over to Ned and called his name.

"What," Ned said without looking over.

"Uh, I wanted to ask you about your book," Nancy said. "Bess Marvin found it in her car."

"No way," Ned said. "I've never been in Bess Marvin's car in my life."

"Really?" Nancy said, thinking hard. "Well, did you—"

But Ned wasn't listening. He had stopped playing catch and was running toward the baseball field.

Hmmm, Nancy thought. Why did he run away? Maybe he didn't want to admit that he'd been in Bess's car.

Nancy scanned the playground to

find Bess and George again. But George was all alone. Nancy ran over to her.

"Where's Bess?" Nancy asked, looking quickly all around.

"She ran inside, crying," George said.

"Why?" Nancy asked.

"She thinks everyone will hate her when they find out the money is gone," George explained.

Oh, no, Nancy thought. She could imagine how Bess felt. Everyone was expecting a gift for Ms. Spencer—and the party was the next day.

"You've got to solve this case today," George pleaded with Nancy. "For Bess's sake."

I know, Nancy thought. For Bess's sake. I've just got to.

6

No Clues

Class, we're going to do something special this afternoon," Ms. Spencer said after lunch. "Take out your journals. I want you to write one paragraph. Describe what you think a wedding should be like."

Nancy reached into her desk. But she didn't take out her journal. She pulled out her special blue detective's notebook instead. She opened it and studied the list of suspects.

Greg. Josh. Rebecca. Ned.

Did she have even one clue about who stole the money from Mrs. Marvin's car?

No. Not one.

That means something, Nancy thought. I usually have *one* clue—at least.

With her favorite blue pen, Nancy doodled and made notes on the page.

First she wrote, "No clues. No clues. No clues."

Beside Rebecca's name she wrote, "Candlesticks?"

Beside Ned Nickerson's name she wrote, "Says he's never been in Bess's car. How did his book get there?"

Beside Greg's and Josh's names she wrote a whole bunch of question marks.

Then Nancy tore off a tiny corner from the page. In her smallest handwriting, she wrote a note to Bess.

"Is Greg riding home with you today?" it said.

Nancy passed it to Bess when Ms. Spencer wasn't looking.

Bess nodded.

Then Nancy tore off another tiny

piece of paper. She wrote, "May I have a ride home?"

Bess nodded again.

Good, Nancy thought as she took out her journal. She started to write her paragraph for Ms. Spencer.

If I ride home with Bess, I can ask Greg where he got the money for those in-line skates. Then maybe I can still solve this mystery before it's too late!

After school Nancy and Bess hurried to the van.

"Do you want me to come, too?" George asked. "We could gang up on him."

"No," Nancy said. "It's better if I ask him myself. He might get mad if we gang up on him."

Nancy and Bess said goodbye to George and started walking toward the car. Nancy's heart began to pound. This is it, she thought. Almost my last chance to solve this case.

The minivan was parked at the edge

of the parking lot. The sliding side door was open. Mrs. Marvin stood outside, talking to some of the other mothers. Bess went over to her mom to say hello.

Greg was already sitting in the backseat. Nancy walked over to the car alone and climbed in. She sat in the middle seat.

"Hi," she said.

"Hi," Greg answered.

Nancy noticed Greg was holding his brand-new in-line skates. They were so shiny, Nancy could see her reflection in them.

"Hey, cool skates," Nancy said. "Where'd you get them?"

"Bought 'em last night. At Skate Escape," Greg said.

"Hmmm," Nancy said. "They look expensive."

"Yeah," Greg said. "They were."

"Where did you get the money?" Nancy asked. She looked Greg right in the eye.

"I got a bunch of money for my

birthday from my grandmother," Greg said. "So I bought them—and my mom couldn't say anything." He gave Nancy a happy grin.

"Cool," Nancy said. But her face fell. She was sure he was telling the truth.

"What's wrong?" Greg asked.

"Oh, nothing," Nancy said.

But when she saw Greg's face, she decided to trust him. Quickly she told him about the missing money.

Greg's face turned bright red.

"What's wrong?" Nancy asked. "Do you know something about it?"

"No," Greg said, shaking his head hard. But Nancy didn't believe him.

"It's just that . . . uh, well, something of mine was stolen yesterday, too," Greg went on.

"What?" Nancy asked.

"A book," Greg said. "A mystery I was reading."

"The one about the detectives?" Nancy asked.

Greg nodded. "It's not even my

book," Greg went on. "It was Ned Nickerson's. He loaned it to me."

Nancy rolled her eyes. So that's it, she thought. That's how Ned's book got into Bess's car.

"Your book wasn't stolen," Nancy said. "You left it in this car. Ask Bess. She has it at her house."

"Really?" Greg said. His face lit up. "Thanks."

Mrs. Marvin and Bess got into the van, and they started on their way home.

Once Greg had been dropped off, Nancy took out her blue notebook. She crossed two names off the suspect list— Greg's and Ned's. But beside Greg's name, she wrote, "He knows something."

Bess started biting her fingernails. "Nancy," she said, "what are we going to do? The party is tomorrow."

Nancy looked at her suspect list again. There was only one real suspect left: Josh.

"Don't worry," Nancy said. "I'm not giving up yet."

When she got home, Nancy ran to the phone in the kitchen. Quickly she dialed Josh Lemon's phone number.

The phone rang five times before Josh picked it up.

"Hi," Nancy said. "May I speak to Josh?"

"Yeah," Josh said. "This is me."

"Oh, hi," Nancy said as sweetly as she could. "This is Nancy Drew. I wanted to ask you—"

But before Nancy could finish her sentence, she heard a loud bang. Then a click.

"I don't believe it," Nancy said. "He hung up on me. That means he must know something. But what?"

7

Party Poopers

What am I going to say?" Bess whispered. "What am I going to tell everyone? They'll hate me."

Nancy, Bess, and George were standing outside Ms. Frick's art room. It was Friday afternoon—the day of the party.

Nancy felt Bess's fingers gripping her arm. They dug in deeper and deeper.

"It will be okay," Nancy said. "Don't worry."

"Yeah," George said. "I'm sure Ms. Frick will help you explain it to the class."

Ms. Frick leaned her head out into the hall and raised her eyebrows. "Coming?" she called to the three girls.

"Come on," Nancy said as she and George pulled Bess toward the classroom. "The bell already rang. We're late."

Bess let out a small moan. But she let Nancy and George lead her toward the art room. The three of them took seats at a table in the very back.

Ms. Frick clapped her hands together. "Well, this is it," she said, smiling. "Party day!"

Everyone let out a cheer.

"Where's the present?" Brenda Carlton called out. She glared at Bess.

"I'll explain about that," Ms. Frick said quickly.

She cleared her throat and waited. When everyone saw the look on her face, they got quiet very fast.

"The money we collected is missing," Ms. Frick said. "It's possible it was stolen from Bess's mother's car."

Nancy watched her classmates closely. A few people gasped. Brenda whirled around and glared at Bess again. So did a few other kids.

"That's terrible!" Lindsay cried out. "What about the cookie jar?"

"It's Bess's fault," Brenda Carlton said loudly. "She should buy the cookie jar with her own money."

Ms. Frick shook her head. She held up her hands for silence.

"No," the art teacher said. "Bess's mother offered to buy it, but I told her not to. It's not the Marvins' fault that the money is missing."

"But the party!" Lindsay cried. "We can't have a party without a present!"

"Yes, we can," Ms. Frick said. "We have the food already. And don't forget—you *made* a present for Ms. Spencer. I'm sure she will treasure that more than anything you could buy."

Ms. Frick pointed to the giant wedding cake card. It was standing open on her desk.

"Don't say a word about the cookie jar," Ms. Frick went on. Then she glanced toward the door. "All right, class, be quiet. Here she comes."

Ms. Spencer walked into the art room. "The principal said you wanted to see me?" she said to Ms. Frick.

"Surprise!" everyone in class called out.

Ms. Spencer blinked. Then she saw the huge wedding card and the food.

The table was spread with little cakes, cookies, and punch. There were even special wedding napkins with silver bells on them.

Ms. Spencer looked totally surprised. She had a huge smile on her face.

"How sweet of you!" she cried.

Nancy grinned and gave Bess's arm a squeeze. "See? Everything's all right," Nancy whispered to her friend.

"How? When . . . ?" Ms. Spencer started to say.

Ms. Frick laughed. "It was the class's idea," she said. "They wanted to do something special for your wedding."

Ms. Frick pointed to the huge card.

"Oh, I love it already," Ms. Spencer said. Nancy and Bess brought it closer.

First Ms. Spencer studied the outside. Then she opened it.

"See the really cool jet planes?" Jason Hutchings called out. "I drew them."

Ms. Spencer laughed. "They're beautiful," she said.

Then she began to read the messages inside.

The first one was a poem from Nancy. It said:

The bride is my teacher.
She's not only smart,
She's also quite beautiful
And has a loving heart.

"Oh, Nancy," Ms. Spencer said, "that's so nice."

By the time Ms. Spencer had read all the poems and messages, she had tears in her eyes.

"This is the best wedding present anyone could give me," she said.

Brenda Carlton cleared her throat. "Well, not really—" she started to say.

Ms. Frick stopped her. "Time for refreshments," the art teacher called.

Noisily, the class pushed back their chairs. Everyone hurried to the table to get cake, cookies, and punch.

Everyone except Bess. She didn't move.

"Come on," Nancy said softly. "Don't be upset anymore. Ms. Spencer's really happy."

"Let's go get some cake," George said.

"I'm not hungry," Bess said.

Nancy and George looked at each other. Bess must have been really upset. She loved sweet things. She *always* wanted cake—whether she was hungry or not.

Nancy and George went to the refreshment table. They chose an extra big piece of cake for Bess.

Bess wouldn't eat it. She wouldn't

even look at it. She just sat at a table by herself, looking glum.

Finally the bell rang. The party was over. School was out for the weekend.

Nancy, Bess, and George walked back to their classroom to get their books from their cubbies.

"Hey, what's this?" Nancy took a folded piece of paper from her cubby.

"Is it a note?" George asked.

"Yes," Nancy answered. She unfolded the note. "Listen to this."

I was fooling around with the money in Bess's car. But I put it back in the envelope. I don't know how it got lost.
Sorry.

Bess put her hands on her hips. " 'Sorry'?" she said, reading the last word. "Hmmph. If the person is so sorry, why didn't he sign his name?"

8

Happily Ever After

At last!" Nancy cried. She clutched the note in her hand and held it up in the air. "I finally have a clue!"

"Huh?" George asked. "How is that a clue? It isn't even signed."

"I know," Nancy said with a smile. "But I think I know who wrote it. Come on!"

Without waiting for Bess and George, Nancy grabbed her backpack. She nearly ran out of the classroom, down the hall, and out of school. By the time she reached the parking lot, she was out of breath.

Nancy scanned the lot. She spotted

the Marvins' red minivan. Greg was standing beside it.

"Hi," Nancy said to Greg. "Look what I found in my cubby." She handed him the note.

Greg looked at it.

"I know," Greg said. "Josh wrote it."

Nancy's eyes grew big. "He did?" she said. "I thought *you* wrote it."

"No," Greg said. "It was Josh. He was fooling around with the envelope on Wednesday. He joked about taking it. But he was just kidding. When Mrs. Marvin came to the car, Josh put it back. I know he did. I saw him."

Nancy closed her eyes for a minute to think.

Josh fooled around with the money. Then he put it back.

"Did you *see* him put it back?" Nancy asked. "In Mrs. Marvin's purse?"

"Yeah," Greg said. "At least I think so. I couldn't really see where he put it. I was in the backseat. But I *know* he didn't take it."

61

Nancy closed her eyes again and thought hard. Then she opened them and took out her notebook. There was something she couldn't remember.

"Oh, yes," Nancy said when she saw the notes she had written on the page. "Now I remember."

"Remember what?" Bess asked as she and George climbed into the car.

"The post office," Nancy said. "You went to the post office on Wednesday. To mail a package to your grandmother. Right?"

Bess nodded.

"Was it that big brown padded envelope? The one on the floor by your mom's purse?" Nancy asked.

"Yes," Bess said. "There was a book in it. And some photos."

"I saw the package," Nancy said, getting excited. "And it was open."

"So what?" Bess and George said at the same time.

"So what? Here's what," Nancy began. "What if Josh didn't put the envelope back in your mom's purse? What if he put it in the package for your grandmother instead—by accident."

Bess's mouth fell open.

"Nancy, you're a genius," George said.

Nancy smiled. "Well?" she asked Bess. "Do you think it could have happened that way?"

"Maybe," Bess said. "But then—"

"Then the money would have been mailed to your grandmother!" Nancy exclaimed.

Bess got out and went to where her mother was standing. Nancy watched while Bess told her mother everything. Then Bess climbed back into the van.

"Mom says you could be right," Bess said. "She didn't have any staples at home, so she couldn't seal the envelope. She had them tape it closed at the post office."

"Yay!" George said, jumping up and down.

"Hey, you really *are* a good detective," Greg said.

"Hold on," Nancy said. "I don't even know if I'm right, yet."

"After your mom drives Greg home, we can go to your house and call your grandmother," George said. "Maybe she's gotten the package in the mail."

As soon as Mrs. Marvin parked the car, the girls ran into Bess's house. Bess made the call. Just as George hoped, the package had arrived that day.

Bess's grandmother opened it—and found the envelope of money inside.

"Mom!" Bess called from the phone. "Grammy's got the money. Can we go buy the schoolhouse cookie jar now?"

Bess's mother came running. She gave Nancy a hug. "Yes," she said, smiling broadly. "Yes, of course. Oh, thank you, Nancy. You've done it again."

The next morning Nancy bubbled with excitement. She had never been to a wedding before. She put on her new flowered dress and brushed her hair. Then Hannah helped her tie her hair back with a matching bow.

"You look scrumptious," Nancy's father said.

Nancy beamed. "Let's go, Daddy," she said. "We've got to pick up Bess and George. I don't want to be late."

Just as Nancy walked out the front door, Rebecca arrived.

"Oh, thank goodness you didn't leave yet!" Rebecca said dramatically. "Here."

She handed Nancy a card.

"What's this?" Nancy asked.

"Well," Rebecca said, blushing. "My mom wouldn't let me buy crystal candlesticks. So I made Ms. Spencer a card myself. With a drawing of candlesticks on the front."

"That was sweet of you," Nancy said.

Rebecca pouted. "I wish I could come," she said softly.

"I wish you could, too," Nancy said

as she hurried to the car and got in. Then, as her dad pulled out of the driveway, Nancy rolled down the window. "I'll bring you some of the mints," she called.

"Mints?" Carson Drew said. "How do you know they'll have mints at the wedding?"

"Rebecca told me," Nancy said with a smile.

Soon they had picked up Bess and George. Carson Drew drove to the church. When they got out of the car, he jumped out, too.

"I just want to take a picture of you three," he said.

Nancy stood between her two best friends. Bess's cheeks glowed. She held the wedding gift—the special cookie jar—in her arms. It was wrapped in silver paper just as Lindsay and Rebecca said it should be.

"You look beautiful," Carson said to the girls.

The wedding ceremony was short,

but Nancy loved every minute of it. Her favorite part was the end. First Ms. Spencer kissed her husband. Then the bride and groom walked down the aisle together. The organ music played.

"I want my wedding to be just like this," Bess said as they hurried to the wedding reception.

That night Nancy lay in her bed with her blue notebook open. She stared at the place where she had written "No clues."

No wonder I couldn't catch the thief, Nancy thought.

There wasn't any thief.

Then Nancy turned to a new page in her notebook. She took out a pen and wrote:

Yesterday I solved the case of the Wedding Gift Goof—and today I went to my first wedding. I also found out something important about presents. We talked Ms.

Spencer into opening our cookie jar gift at the wedding. And guess what? She said she liked the present we made for her just as much as the one we bought. I guess that means we didn't goof up after all.

Case closed.

FULL HOUSE™

Michelle

#1: THE GREAT PET PROJECT 51905-0/$3.50

#2: THE SUPER-DUPER 51906-9/$3.50
SLEEPOVER PARTY

#3: MY TWO BEST FRIENDS 52271-X/$3.50

#4: LUCKY, LUCKY DAY 52272-8/$3.50

#5: THE GHOST IN MY CLOSET 53573-0/$3.50

#6: BALLET SURPRISE 53574-9/$3.50

#7: MAJOR LEAGUE TROUBLE 53575-7/$3.50

#8: MY FOURTH-GRADE MESS 53576-5/$3.50

#8: BUNK 3, TEDDY, AND ME 56834-5/$3.50

A MINSTREL® BOOK

Published by Pocket Books

Simon & Schuster Mail Order Dept. BWB
200 Old Tappan Rd., Old Tappan, N.J. 07675

Please send me the books I have checked above. I am enclosing $_____(please add $0.75 to cover the postage and handling for each order. Please add appropriate sales tax). Send check or money order--no cash or C.O.D.'s please. Allow up to six weeks for delivery. For purchase over $10.00 you may use VISA: card number, expiration date and customer signature must be included.

Name _____

Address _____

City _____ State/Zip _____

VISA Card # _____ Exp.Date _____

Signature _____

TAKE A RIDE
WITH THE KIDS ON BUS FIVE!

Natalie Adams and James Penny have just started
third grade. They like their teacher, and they like
Maple Street School. The only trouble is, they have
to ride bad old Bus Five to get there!

#1 THE BAD NEWS BULLY
Can Natalie and James stop the bully on Bus Five?
Coming mid-July '96

#2 WILD MAN AT THE WHEEL
When Mr. Balter calls in sick,
the kids get some strange new drivers.
Coming mid-August '96

#3 FINDERS KEEPERS
The kids on Bus Five keep losing things.
Is there a thief on board?
Coming mid-September '96

#4 I SURVIVED ON BUS FIVE
Bad luck turns into big fun
when Bus Five breaks down in a rainstorm.
Coming mid-October '96

BY MARCIA LEONARD
ILLUSTRATED BY JULIE DURRELL

A MINSTREL® BOOK

Published by Pocket Books

1237